ULTIMATE STICKER

DINOSAURS

Have fun completing the dinosaur sticker and coloring activities! Pull out the sticker sheets and keep them by you when you complete each sticker activity page. There are also extra stickers to use throughout this book or anywhere you want!

make believe ideas

Dinosaur tour!

Color in the vehicles and find the missing stickers.

3

Amazing maze

Follow the maze to help Stegosaurus Sam find his friend.

Start

Finish

Dino drawings

Use stickers and color to complete the dinosaurs.

Run, run!

Join the numbers to see
who's scaring the dinosaurs!

6
7
8
5
9
4
10
3
11
2
12
1
46
45
44
43
42
41
40
39
38
37
36
35
34
33
32
31
30
29
28
27
26
25
24
23
22
21
20
19
18
17
16
15
14
13

Dino wordsearch

Hunt for the dino words in the wordsearch.

- ○ fossil
- ○ dinosaur
- ○ claws
- ○ bone
- ○ roar
- ○ dig
- ○ skull
- ○ fern
- ○ horn
- ○ bite
- ○ egg
- ○ Trex

S	A	L	C	L	A	W	S	O	P
K	M	H	O	N	B	U	T	R	N
U	F	O	S	S	I	L	U	V	M
L	O	R	M	R	O	A	R	L	D
L	H	N	Y	E	S	O	V	E	F
G	O	X	Q	O	B	K	J	O	B
G	I	D	N	N	I	O	N	T	O
E	O	I	R	U	T	L	K	R	N
O	O	D	O	N	R	E	F	O	E
X	H	Z	E	J	C	S	A	X	H

Dinosaur games

Color and sticker the dinosaurs having fun!

How to draw a dinosaur!

1 Grab a pencil and paper and draw an oval.

2 Draw a triangle for a tail.

3 Draw another oval for the head.

4 Draw a neck.

5 Draw two rectangles as legs.

6 Draw triangles on the head, back, and tail, then color in your dinosaur!

Dino dinnertime

Find the missing stickers in the dinosaur fridge.

Write and sticker Terry T. rex's favorite snack!

....

Yum!

Dinosaur holiday

Greetings from Eygpt

Write or draw on the postcard, then sticker the stamp!

Dear Auntie Diplodocus,

Dino surfing!

Derek Dino is going surfing!
Color and sticker the surfboard.

Discover a dinosaur!

Draw and color the latest dinosaur
you have discovered.

You can use
stickers, too!

Copycat dinos

Copy the pictures. Use the grids to help you!

How many bones can you count on this page? ....

Dotty discovery!

Color the dotted sections red to see who's hiding!

Dino pool party!

Find the missing stickers and add color to the dino party.

19

Dinos in disguise!

Use your stickers to disguise the dinosaurs.

20

Egg-citing trails!

Find the missing stickers and follow the trails
to see which egg belongs to each dinosaur.

Deep-space dinos!

Use stickers and color to
complete the space scene.

Circle the planet
that doesn't belong.

Design my flag!

Sticker more footprints!

23

Prehistoric party!

Use stickers to help the dinos dress up!

Mix and match!

The dino babies are mixed up! Follow the trails
to see which baby belongs to each mom.
Then color them to match!

Cook-off!

Read the recipe and sticker the right ingredients in the bowls.

4 strawberries

3 oranges

2 pieces of broccoli

Deep-sea divers

Use stickers and color to complete
the underwater scene.

Who's in the submarine?

Find the missing stickers and circle the fish that doesn't belong.

29

Dinosaur fun!

Find the missing stickers to complete the patterns.

How many bones can you count?

Answer

....

Copy the dino baby! Use the grid to help you.

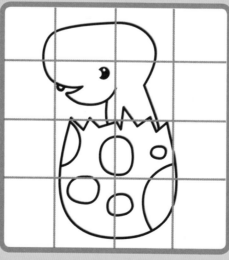

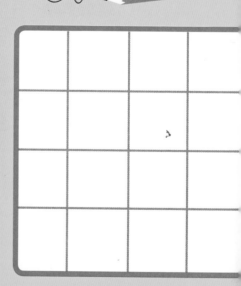

Look closely!

Circle the one that does not belong in each row.

Dino maths

Can you help T. rex count? Find the
missing stickers and trace the numbers.

I love counting!

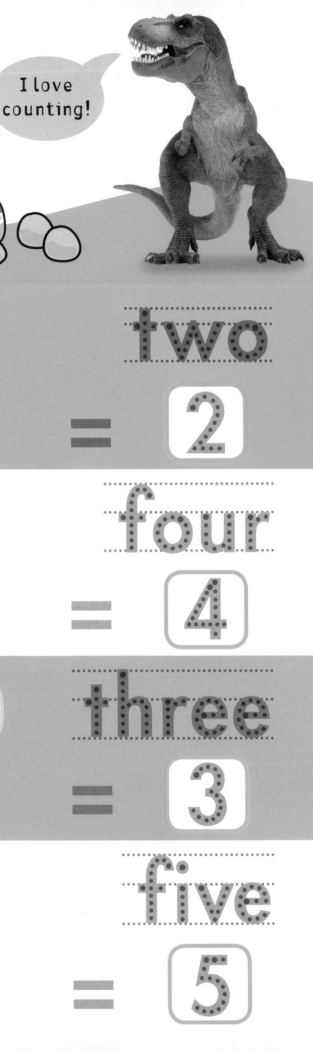

1 + 1 = **two** 2

2 + 2 = **four** 4

1 + 2 = **three** 3

3 + 2 = **five** 5

Hide and seek!

Sticker the baby dinosaurs hiding in the cave.

Ready, steady, go!

Who won the race? Find the missing stickers and color in the rosettes.

Wait for me!

YAY!

35

Rumble, grumble!

What do the hungry dinosaurs like eating?
Sticker food in their tummies!

Busy counting

How many can you count? Find the missing stickers, then write your answers in the circles provided.

Trees

Bones

Eggs

Footprints

Number fun

Find the missing stickers, count
the objects, and trace the numbers.

RAAAAR!

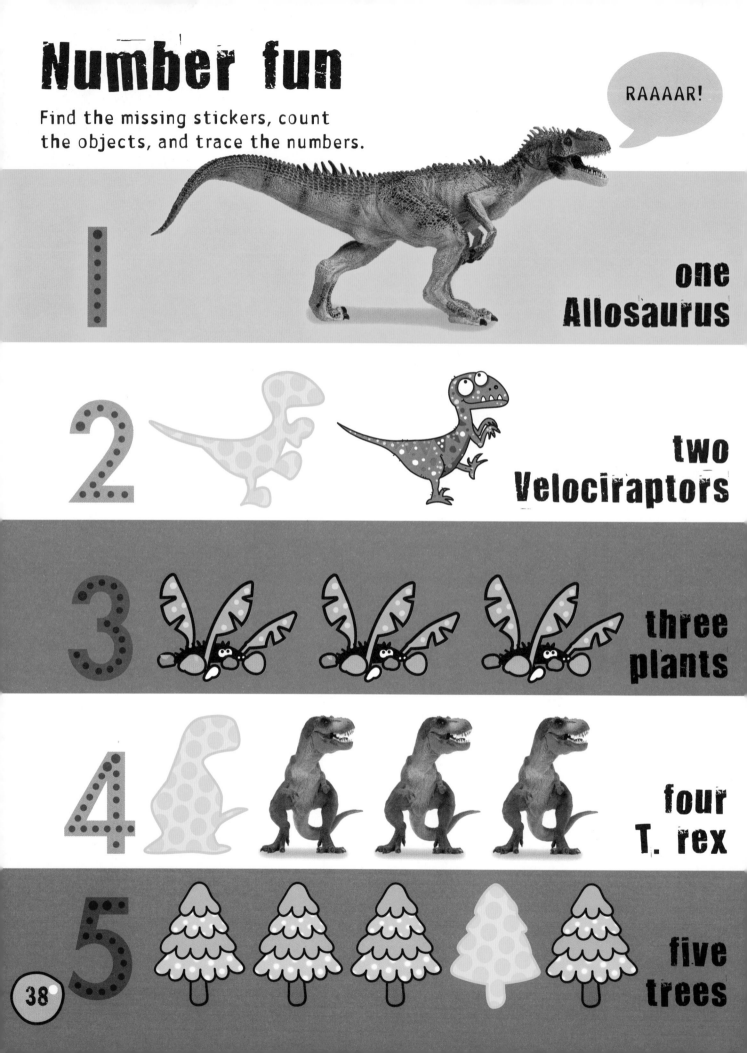

1 one
Allosaurus

2 two
Velociraptors

3 three
plants

4 four
T. rex

5 five
trees

6 six footprints

7 seven flowers

8 eight bones

9 nine rocks

10 ten eggs

39

Spot the difference!

Find and circle 6 differences between the two pictures.

Stickers for pages 2-3

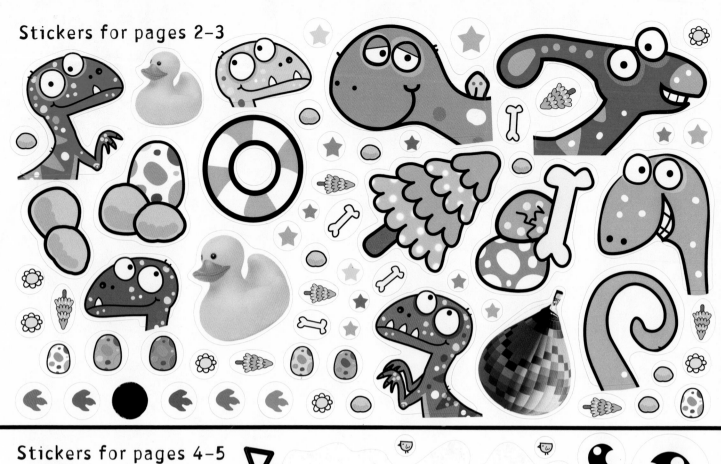

Stickers for pages 4-5

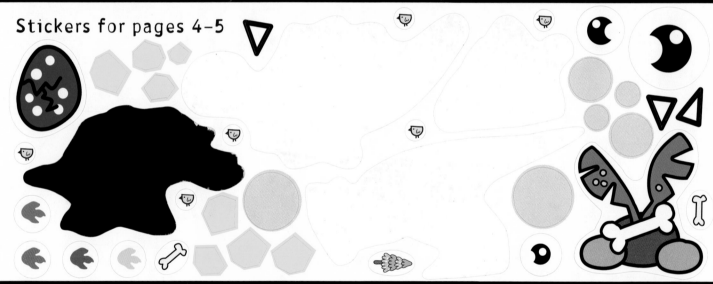

Stickers for pages 6-7

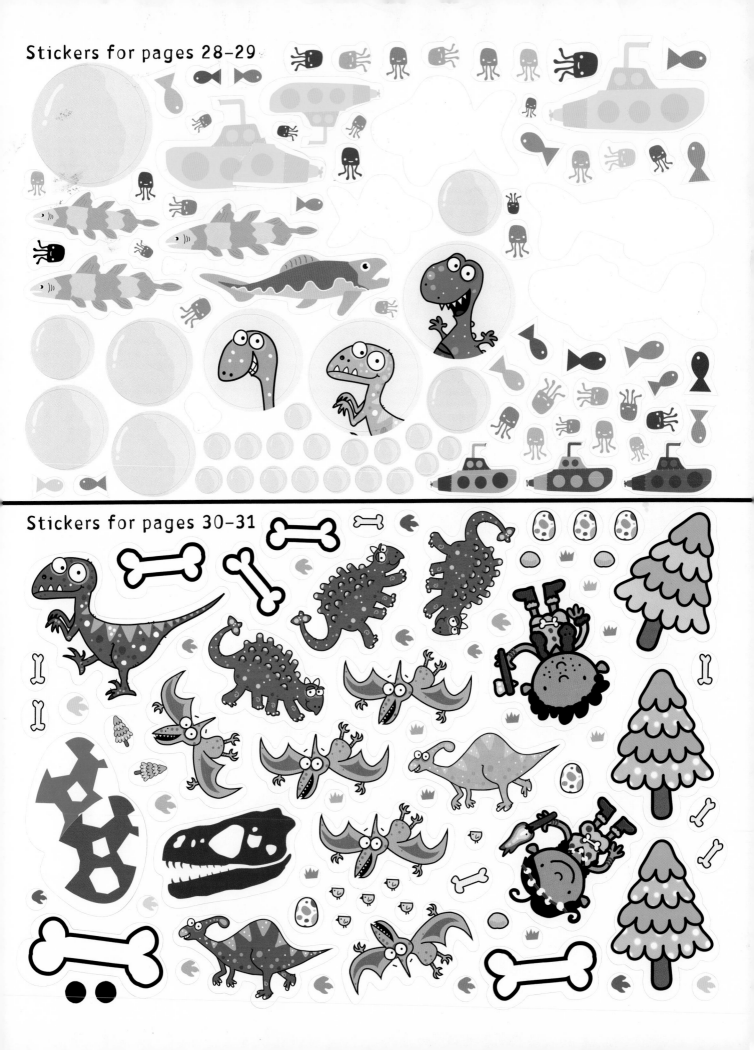

Stickers for pages 28-29

Stickers for pages 30-31

Stickers for pages 32–33

Stickers for pages 34–35

1st 2nd 3rd

Stickers for pages 36–37

Stickers for pages 38–39